Bantam Books in the Choose Your Own Adventure® Series
Ask your bookseller for the books you have missed.

SOUTH POLE SABOTAGE

BY SEDDON JOHNSON

ILLUSTRATED BY FRANK BOLLE

An R.A. Montgomery Book

BANTAM BOOKS
TORONTO • NEW YORK • LONDON • SYDNEY • AUCKLAND

RL 5, IL age 10 and up

SOUTH POLE SABOTAGE
A Bantam Book / March 1989

CHOOSE YOUR OWN ADVENTURE® is a registered trademark of
Bantam Books, a division of Bantam Doubleday Dell Publishing Group, Inc.
Registered in U.S. Patent and Trademark Office and elsewhere.

Original conception of Edward Packard

Interior illustrations by Frank Bolle
Cover art by Romas Kukalis

ISBN 0-553-27770-7

Published simultaneously in the United States and Canada

Bantam Books are published by Bantam Books, a division of Bantam Doubleday
Dell Publishing Group, Inc. Its trademark, consisting of the words "Bantam
Books" and the portrayal of a rooster, is Registered in U.S. Patent and Trademark
Office and in other countries. Marca Registrada. Bantam Books, 666 Fifth Ave-
nue, New York, New York 10103.

PRINTED IN THE UNITED STATES OF AMERICA

O   0 9 8 7 6 5 4 3 2 1

With love, to Zenita Coates

WARNING!!!

Do not read this book straight through from beginning to end! These pages contain many different adventures you may have when you travel to the Antarctic aboard your uncle's ocean research vessel to investigate a hole in the Earth's ozone layer.

From time to time as you read along you will have to make choices and decisions. Your choices may lead to success or disaster. The adventures that follow are the results of your choices.

Be careful! Your expedition aboard the *Pole Star* will bring you face to face with some scientists who desperately want to sabotage your expedition!

Good luck!

Your uncle Ben owns the ocean research vessel *Pole Star*, and this summer the United Nations chartered the ship for one month. The *Pole Star* will be traveling south to the Antarctic to investigate a hole in the Earth's protective ozone layer, and you'll be going with them. Uncle Ben has told you that the mission is of the greatest importance. Less than a month ago, a United Nations satellite, which checked the ozone layer automatically, mysteriously disappeared from orbit without leaving a trace. The *Pole Star* expedition must set up a monitoring station near the South Pole to take over these studies until a new satellite can be launched.

You don't know much about the ozone layer. But as you go over the plans of the expedition with your uncle Ben, he explains more to you.

"Ozone," he says, "is a gas related to oxygen. Imagine that the planet Earth is the yolk of an egg and the egg white is our atmosphere, the stuff we breathe. Then think of the ozone layer as the shell of the egg—a kind of protective cover. Think what would happen if the shell had a hole in it!"

Turn to page 4.

The ledge is only a few meters below you, and you're almost sure that you'll land on it.

It takes you only a few seconds to cut through the nylon line. You fall, and as you land on the ledge, your head smashes against the ice. You see stars. You've lost your ice axe. As you begin to slip slowly off the ice shelf, you desperately try to dig your nails in to prevent from slipping—but it's too late. You slip farther, then fall, tumbling downward into the icy black depths for what seems like an eternity. And it is.

The End

About half an hour later, you suddenly notice that the clear blue sky has become hazy, and the ground below you is disappearing into a mush of white swirling clouds. Whiteout! Without a horizon to orient you, your head spins, all sense of direction gone. You won't even be able to see . . .

The End

"You mean that our atmosphere would leak out?" you ask, astonished.

Uncle Ben shakes his head. "No, but just as bad. Dangerous ultraviolet rays would leak in. The ozone layer filters out most of the harmful ultraviolet rays that come from the sun. Without a protective shell of ozone, all the crops in the world could burn up. All the people and animals of planet Earth could develop deadly skin diseases. And eventually, the global temperature would rise, melting the polar ice caps. That would raise the level of the oceans of the world by more than six meters and flood coastal cities such as New York, Buenos Aires, Tokyo, and Sydney."

Until your uncle Ben explained the importance of the ozone layer, you thought this trip would be dull. But now you realize that the future of the world may depend on the success of this expedition. And you're an important member of it!

"Now get to work," Uncle Ben orders. "We've got a lot to do before we leave."

Turn to page 8.

You pick yourself up and sprint the final hundred meters to the thick ice floe where your crew warmly congratulates you on your close escape.

After a restless night, you awake to a warm morning sun. It feels good not to be freezing for a change, but Scotty points out that the ice floe is rapidly melting. Pools of water have formed, and the edges of the floe are starting to break away.

Ocean swells are heaving your ice floe up and down, making it creak from the pressure. Alarmed, you post a guard to keep watch for any cracks and order that all the equipment should be loaded in the lifeboats just in case the floe splits in half.

A little after noon, the guard screams, "It's starting to crack. The floe is breaking up!"

If you launch the lifeboats and desert the ice floe, turn to page 40.

If you move the crew and equipment to the larger part of the floe, turn to page 33.

Once the expedition is gone, you strut around on deck. Being second mate is terrific, and even the cook salutes you. But that night, you find out what having the responsibility of an officer means. A fierce northerly storm starts to blow into the bay, and the lookout reports that the anchor is dragging. Mr. Bannon rushes forward to check, but he slips and falls, hitting his head hard against the deck. His limp body is quickly taken down to the ship's hospital. He regains consciousness a few minutes later, but the doctor insists that he stay in the infirmary for at least a day.

You realize you're in charge now! And the wind is rapidly rising to hurricane force. You're faced with an important decision.

If you let the anchor drag, the *Pole Star* will drift ashore onto the sandy beach and go aground. Then you can wait until the wind subsides and, with any luck, back off safely into deep water.

Or you can raise anchor and take your chances on riding out the storm. Either way, it's going to be a sleepless and dangerous night.

If you decide to raise the anchor and ride out the storm, turn to page 18.

If you let the anchor drag the Pole Star *ashore, turn to page 16.*

8

The *Pole Star* is a modern steel vessel, seventy meters long, and built for extended cruising in the polar regions. She has been "down to the ice" many times before. One of your closest friends is the engineering officer, "Scotty" MacTagget, a Scottish man who has been with the *Pole Star* since she was launched on the River Clyde in Scotland more than seventeen years ago.

Scotty has taught you a lot about the ship's machinery, and Uncle Ben has tutored you in navigation and ship handling. You hope that someday, after you graduate from school, you can be a ship's officer and maybe, eventually, a captain.

All afternoon, scientific equipment, food, drums of gasoline, and snowmobiles are loaded on deck. Then, by evening, the leader of the expedition, Dr. Pogolsky, a world-famous Polish scientist, arrives. He is accompanied by two young assistants— Jozef and Marie.

In the early morning hours, a tug nudges the *Pole Star* from her berth, and she moves out of Invercargill, New Zealand, setting a course south toward the Antarctic into the teeth of a rising gale. Your adventure has begun.

Turn to page 31.

Once the towline is cut, you head the *Pole Star* offshore, right into the storm. As the hours pass, the waves become gigantic, the wind grows fierce, and the *Pole Star* begins to groan as her hull is repeatedly smashed by the seas that roar down on her like express trains.

Sometime in the early morning, Scotty calls you on the intercom. "The patches on the hull are leaking badly, skipper. They look like they'll let go any minute."

Bad news!

And just then, you spot a monster wave, huger than all the rest. It towers over the *Pole Star* and finally breaks in a cascade of white water. The impact shatters all the windows on the bridge deck. Seawater immediately starts to flood in.

Turn to page 20.

The killer whales roll over on the surface, their black eyes glaring at you. Then they slide below the water. Just when you think they've gone and left you alone, the whales leap out of the water on their tails and take an even closer look at you!

Suddenly you realize that in your black exposure suit, you must look like a plump and delicious young seal—their favorite meal!

If you try to outmaneuver the whales by jumping from floe to floe, turn to page 27.

If you decide to trick the whales by playing dead, turn to page 25.

Just looking at the names on the chart sends chills down your spine: *Thunderclap Glacier, Skull Mountains, Danger Bay.* This isn't going to be any picnic!

"We'll unload the equipment on the ice shelf," says Uncle Ben, "then anchor in Danger Bay."

You look at the itinerary as your uncle instructs the crew. Dr. Pogolsky's group will head south on their snowmobiles to Camp One and spend the night there. The next day they'll speed on to Camp Two on Mount Gay in the Rhumb Mountains. There they will set up their automatic ozone-monitoring equipment and then head back to the *Pole Star.* "I've decided to go with Dr. Pogolsky's party," says Uncle Ben. "I'm familiar with the Antarctic, and they will need my help."

"But who'll be in charge of the *Pole Star* while you're gone?" you ask.

"First Mate Bannon, of course," replies Uncle Ben. "You can either stay aboard as temporary second mate or join the expedition as cook."

Being promoted to temporary second mate is quite an honor, you think, as you consider what to do. But being part of the expedition and seeing the Antarctic firsthand would be really exciting.

If you decide to join the expedition, turn to page 44.

If you want to become temporary second mate, turn to page 6.

A man in a hat with gold braiding appears in the conning tower. "Ahoy," he calls through a megaphone. "Who are you, and where are you from?"

You cup your hands around your mouth and shout back, "From the research vessel *Pole Star.* We had an accident and had to abandon ship. Who are you, and where are you from?"

"The submarine *Terror.* Captain Hawk in command. And where we're from is none of your business."

You gulp. The *Terror* and her skipper are not exactly the rescuers you had in mind.

"I'll save you and your party on three conditions," Captain Hawk's voice booms across the water. "First of all," he says, "you cannot use my radio to notify anyone that you're safe. My position and the identity of my submarine must remain secret. Second, because some of my men are incapacitated with food poisoning, I'm short of crew. You and your people must swear loyalty to me and join my crew. You'll do as you're told; no arguments and no excuses. And finally, I have a mission to perform that has priority over putting you ashore. You will serve me until that mission is completed. After that, I'll drop all of you off on an island in the South Atlantic, and from there you can make your way home."

If you accept Captain Hawk's proposal, turn to page 36.

If you decide to keep heading for the Soviet base, turn to page 38.

14

You maneuver the *Pole Star* alongside a large ice floe and order food, tents, sleeping bags, and cooking fuel to be loaded into the lifeboats. Then you lower them directly onto the ice.

Scotty runs up the ladder to the bridge. His face is blackened with soot, and his hair is singed. "She's going to blow up any minute, skipper. We've got to get off her right now."

You know that if the *Pole Star* blows up near the ice floe, the explosion could break up the floe as well as kill whoever is left on board. You've got to get her at least a kilometer away from here before you can leave the ship.

"Abandon ship, Scotty. I'll move her away from the ice floe and then row back in the dinghy." You change into your black exposure suit in preparation for the dangerous and frigid row ahead.

Turn to page 26.

16

You let the anchor drag. The wind howls. Spume blown by the wind turns the bay into a froth of white. You hope that after the wind dies, you'll be able to back the *Pole Star* out of the sandy cove under the power of her engines. But your plans are shattered as the hull grates over underwater rocks.

Scotty calls up from the engine room. "The bottom's ripped out of her," he shouts into the intercom. "The water level is already up over the engines. We're going down."

Sinking?!

Turn to page 22.

Through the long, stormy night, the *Miska* tows you toward the Soviet research station. It's dangerous, but because of the skill of the Soviet captain, everything goes well—until a little after noon.

All at once you hear a loud *thud,* and the *Miska* shudders violently, then slowly begins to sink. You hear the shouts of the Soviet crew to abandon ship, but by the time you reach the lifeboats, they're all gone!

The End

You and the *Pole Star* ride out the storm through the harrowing night.

By the next morning, the storm is over. You're exhausted but looking forward to a good rest once you get back to Danger Bay. Then Scotty unexpectedly calls on the intercom.

"Skipper—a fuel line broke, and we've got a wee bit of a fire down here in the engine room. I'll keep you up-to-date on how the crew and I are handling it."

Fire! The very thought strikes fear into any ship's captain. And this is your first command.

Scotty calls back in twenty minutes. "Sorry, skipper, but the flames are out of control. I've got to order everyone to evacuate the engine room—right now!"

This means that you've got to give the order to abandon ship. You send out a radio distress call, but there's no answer. You suspect that the radio antenna was broken during the storm. With no other ship coming to the rescue, you and your crew will be on your own.

Go on to the next page.

There is a pack of ice floes only a few miles south. You might be able to pull alongside one of the larger ones and unload your crew, the lifeboats, and survival gear. But you also remember that it's early summer in the Antarctic and the ice floes will be breaking up. You might be a lot safer in the lifeboats.

If you unload your crew and equipment onto one of the floes, turn to page 14.

If you order your crew to launch the lifeboats, turn to page 40.

The helmsman is knocked out cold when the wave slams him against the bulkhead. Without anyone to steer her, the *Pole Star* turns broadside to the seas and wind. You grab the helm and steer the ship.

As the *Pole Star* struggles to shake off the tons of water, you have a chance to check for damage. Horrified, you look at the forward deck. A huge split has developed, and the bow has broken away from the rest of the hull!

"Close all watertight doors," you bellow into the intercom.

Scotty frantically replies that the watertight doors are collapsing and a flood of water is filling up the engine room.

The *Pole Star* is sinking, and there's nothing you can do to save her.

The End

There are fifteen crew members aboard, and they're your responsibility! You pick up the microphone of the powerful shortwave radio and yell, *"Mayday!"*—the international distress signal for ships in danger.

Within seconds, you receive two answers crackling back through the static. One is from the Soviet research station MIR, and the other is from the small New Zealand weather observation station KIWI.

KIWI station is 600 kilometers to the west. They can't send any overland help. Their weather forecasters are predicting that another storm is building up in the South Atlantic and will hit before they can possibly get there. But they tell you that a rescue plane can fly directly in from New Zealand to help evacuate your crew. And it can land on the ice shelf next to Danger Bay within twenty-four hours.

MIR (which you know from your Russian Language studies in school means "peace") is a lot closer. They offer to send the Soviet icebreaker *Miska* to help savage the *Pole Star.* The *Miska* can be alongside the *Pole Star* by tomorrow afternoon—about twelve hours' time.

If you ask the New Zealanders at KIWI base to send a rescue airlift, turn to page 32.

If you call the Soviet base, turn to page 28.

You push a dinghy overboard and jump in after it. The cold of the water knifes through you, but you quickly scramble aboard. Then you look back to see the *Pole Star* slide beneath the waves and disappear in a flurry of foam.

You start to row toward the crew of the *Pole Star* as they frantically wave at you from their ice floe about two kilometers away. Then you realize you'll never make it. The dinghy has a gaping hole in the bottom, and it's sinking!

You make it to a jumble of pack ice, abandon the dinghy, and start to jump from one floe to the next, heading toward your crew. It's not easy going: some of the floes are lumpy, and others are very thin, sometimes cracking underfoot. At last you come to a large expanse of black water that you can't leap across. You're about to retrace your steps when three large fins break the surface, heading for you.

Killer whales!

Turn to page 11.

You moan and groan, trying to convince the killer whales that you really are a dying seal. Your voice slowly trails off into a long sigh. You hold your breath, waiting.

The floe tips a little, and out of the corner of your eye, you can see a killer whale resting its head on the edge of the ice, staring at you. Then the floe tips a bit more, and now there are two whales, side by side, eyeing you hungrily.

Maybe they're not such fussy eaters after all.

Suddenly a dozen or so Adélie penguins leap onto your ice floe, unaware of the presence of the killer whales. They waddle around, nudging you with their bills, cackling to each other. Then they spot the killer whales. The penguins take off as fast as commuters running for the last train and dive into the sea. The whales take off after the penguins like sleek, black-and-white torpedoes.

Turn to page 5.

Once Scotty has slid down a rope to the ice, you use the last of the power in the engines to back the *Pole Star* away from the floe.

There is no time to spare. Already flames are belching out of the cargo hold, and the steel decks are glowing red hot.

You've managed to steam several kilometers away from the ice floe when you hear a deep rumble in the guts of the ship, followed by a thunderous explosion that knocks you off your feet.

Turn to page 23.

You start running as fast as you can, leaping from one ice floe to the next, not daring to take the time to even look back.

You are very close to the ice floe where your crew is waving and cheering you on. The final stretch is a sheet of fairly thin ice. You hope it's strong enough to support your weight.

You're panting now—only a hundred meters to go. But then the ice heaves up from beneath you and shatters into a thousand fragments. The killer whales have been tracking your shadow on the ice and have smashed the thin layer to get at you!

Splash! You fall into the black water. The last thing you see is a gaping mouth filled with very large, very sharp, pearly white teeth.

The End

You tell the Soviets to send the icebreaker *Miska*. All through the night, you and the crew desperately pump out the seawater that is flooding into the *Pole Star*'s hull. By early morning, the water is low enough for Scotty to get both of the engines operating and hook up the pumps. You haven't slept in twenty-four hours, but you still pace up and down the deck, anxiously looking out to sea for the *Miska*'s arrival.

Then, in the last rays of sunlight as storm clouds blot out the horizon, the *Miska* steams into Danger Bay, her horn hooting and the seamen on deck waving. She's not much larger than the *Pole Star*, but she's a proud ship, run by a brave crew. You know that these people are risking their lives to come to your aid.

Quickly the *Miska* ties up alongside the *Pole Star*, and teams of workers swarm aboard your ship. Within a few hours, they have welded temporary steel patches over the rips in your hull, and then, using a steel cable, they pull the *Pole Star* off the rocks.

Go on to the next page.

The winds from the new storm are already whistling through the rigging as you are towed out to sea. The Soviet captain radios to suggest that she can tow you down the coast to the Soviet research station MIR, where permanent repairs can be made. But you worry about the approaching storm. If the towline breaks, both ships could be quickly driven into the ice pack and sink. Maybe it would be better to cast off the towline and head both ships into deeper water where they would be safer. You radio back and explain the situation to the Soviet captain, and she bravely says that it's up to you.

If you radio the Miska *to keep towing, turn to page 17.*

If you cut the towline and head offshore into deeper water, turn to page 9.

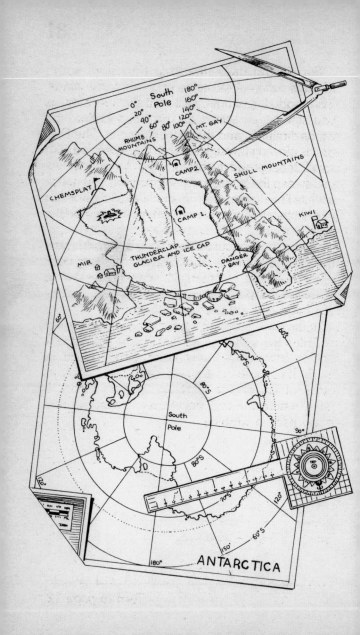

For several days, the *Pole Star* slogs south through mountainous seas and gale-force winds. Everybody is feeling seasick, but one morning, as you stand your watch on the ship's bridge, the winds diminish, and the sun breaks out. The *Pole Star* is plowing through smooth seas speckled with small icebergs and the broken mush of pack ice. As you sweep the horizon with binoculars, you notice a white line that spans from one end of the horizon to the other. Quickly you call down to your uncle, and he comes up to the bridge.

Taking the binoculars from you, he slowly scans the southern horizon, then nods, confirming your opinion. Ahead, less than twenty kilometers away, is Thunderclap Glacier and Ice Cap—the northern edge of the Antarctic continent.

In the chart room, Uncle Ben shows you a chart of Antarctica and explains that it is the highest and coldest continent—and the most remote place on earth. It is far colder than the Arctic and perhaps even colder than the surface of the planet Mars! A place where the sun never sets in summer and never rises in winter!

Turn to page 12.

You instruct the New Zealanders to send in their rescue plane. As morning approaches, the wind calms down, and by noon, you and Scotty are able to launch the lifeboats and ferry the crew ashore, where you set up shelters and a food kitchen.

The plane should have arrived by noon, and you're getting nervous. Although the wind is calm, black clouds are building up to the north, and the second storm will hit within just a few hours.

Then a gleaming silver plane sweeps over the *Pole Star,* waggling its wings to let you know that you've been seen. The twin-engined plane enters a steep bank, then lowers its skis and lands. The rugged New Zealand pilots tell you that they'll come back to pick up Dr. Pogolsky and the rest of the onshore group in five days. Right now, it's time to get out before the next storm breaks.

As the plane takes off and climbs, you look back at the *Pole Star.* When the next storm arrives, she'll be battered to death on the rocks. You were her captain for less than a day, and you lost her! Maybe you should take off your gold braid, forget about going to sea, and become an accountant instead. Then the only ship you'll lose will be the rowboat you rent on a Sunday afternoon at the park.

The End

"Everyone and everything onto the larger floe," you yell. Working like demons, the crew pushes one of the lifeboats across the widening crack. But when you try to move the second boat across, the gap has grown wider. A few of you, reeling back from the break in the ice, find yourselves separated from the others by black and frigid water.

"We'll throw lines across," Scotty yells. And with a strenuous effort, with all of you tugging, you're able to pull the two ice floes close enough together to slide the second lifeboat across and leap over the gap.

Everyone is relieved when it's all over.

After an ample dinner, everyone crawls into sleeping bags for the night.

In the early morning hours, you are jolted awake. The whole ice floe is trembling, and you hear an explosive CRACK. The last thing you feel is water pouring into your sleeping bag.

The End

It's too late to do anything. By the time the cable is repaired, the submarine will be far deeper than she was designed to dive. Her hull will crack like an eggshell, and tons of water will pour in.

As you all watch the depth gauge drop, leaks in pipes and fittings start to spit high-pressure streams of salt water. The hull groans from the tremendous pressure, then suddenly caves in, and a sledgehammer wall of water smashes you. . . .

The End

You and your crew board the *Terror* and are herded down below to the messroom by armed sailors. Captain Hawk stomps in and demands silence.

"You will follow my orders. One of my armed guards will be with you at all times. If you disobey him, you will be shot. Are there any questions?"

You don't like the captain's imperious words and struggle to control your temper . . . and your curiosity. "We owe you our thanks for saving us," you say. "Now that we've joined your crew, please tell us what all this secrecy is about."

Hawk pulls his hand through his beard, smiling. "All right, you'd find out anyway soon enough. A multinational corporation called Chemsplat has developed a laser that is infinitely more powerful than any on Earth. We know they have established a secret underground base right here in the Antarctic—on a plateau by the Thunderclap Ice Cap—so they can test the laser without anyone's knowing. A month ago they demonstrated the power of this deadly laser by vaporizing a United Nations satellite that was measuring the hole in the ozone layer."

"But what exactly is your mission?" you ask.

Go on to the next page.

"The KGB are trying to get to the Chemsplat base before we do." His expression hardens to one of determination. "But we're going to beat them to Chemsplat. The *Terror* will now submerge and run under the ice shelf. When we get to within two kilometers of where the Chemsplat base is, I'll launch some special torpedoes that will break up the ice over the *Terror* and then surface. Then my crew and yours will attack the Chemsplat base."

"Hey—wait a minute!" you snap back at Hawk. "We're here in the Antarctic on a peaceful scientific mission. My crew and I aren't going to attack anyone."

Captain Hawk nods to the guard, who raises his submachine gun. "You'll do as you're told," he says ominously. With that, he and his guard turn and leave the messroom, locking the door behind them.

Turn to page 42.

"Thanks, but no thanks," you angrily shout back at Captain Hawk. "We're heading for the Soviet research station MIR, and they'll take care of us."

"Aha!" Captain Hawk accuses. "I've been shadowing the *Pole Star* for three days, suspecting that you and your so-called research expedition were working for the Soviet secret intelligence service—the KGB."

He then shouts down to his crew who are manning the guns. "All right men—just as I told you. They're foreign spies. Shoot them!"

Suddenly the guns of the *Terror* pour out a stream of deadly fire. Bullets and cannon shells whistle past, then begin to find their mark. In just a few seconds, it's all over.

Those of you still alive can see the fins of sharks closing in.

The End

You and your crew descend stairs cut from ice, the walls and ceiling shored up with heavy wooden planks. At the bottom is a steel door. You ease it open. A blast of hot air washes over you, and the corridor beyond is much like the interior of the *Pole Star*: steel bulkheads painted gray, overhead pipes marked with codes to identify their function, and an anteroom that contains several dozen suits of heavy winter clothing. A low hum from some hidden generator vibrates in the air. All of you huddle over steel grates that emit hot air and slowly warm up. Then, following you, your crew heads down the corridor. At the end of the corridor are three steel doors. One is marked Control Room, another Power Generation Room and the third Laboratory.

"Which way?" asks Scotty as the others look at you expectantly.

You don't want to split up your group. Any one of these three doors sounds as if it would lead to where the operators of this mysterious research facility can be found.

If you enter the control room, turn to page 55.

If you try the power generation room, turn to page 62.

If you explore the laboratory, turn to page 95.

Quickly you and your crew put to sea in the lifeboats. You row your way through the pack ice until you're clear, then hoist the sails. Your plan is to head for the Soviet base. After you arrive, you can contact Dr. Pogolsky's expedition on the Soviets' radio and explain the loss of the *Pole Star* to Uncle Ben. The humiliation is tempered by the fact that you and your crew are safe.

You sail on into the late afternoon. For the Antarctic, the temperature is warm, and you're enjoying the sail. If the winds hold steady and you don't have any more storms, you should be at the Soviet base by this time tomorrow.

Turn to page 50.

In hushed voices, you and your crew discuss your situation. Everyone agrees that there's no way Captain Hawk is going to use the *Pole Star* crew to attack anything.

Scotty has helped you out of trouble before. You hope he can figure a way out of this mess, too.

"What do you think?" you ask Scotty.

"Well," he says, stroking his chin. "This submarine runs on batteries when it's submerged. We could wait until Hawk torpedoes the ice and surfaces. Then, at the last moment, we'd pour salt water on the batteries. That causes chlorine—a poisonous gas—to form. Everyone would have to abandon the *Terror*. We'd know what was happening, and we'd be the first ones out. Then we'd make our getaway and go to the Chemsplat base and get help."

"I've got a better idea," Hans, the bosun, whispers. "See these cables?" He points to very heavy wires running through pulleys. "These run to the rudder. All we have to do is cut them, and the *Terror* will turn in circles. Captain Hawk has us locked in here, but we can also lock him out. We'll be able to negotiate a truce in return for having him drop us off at the Soviet base." Everyone looks at you for your decision.

If you decide to go with Scotty's plan, turn to page 46.

If you decide to cut the cables, turn to page 71.

You and your crew pull desperately on the handles, but the doors won't open. They've been locked from the outside!

Set into one of the walls is a thick glass window. Behind that, a bespectacled face leers out at you, grinning insanely. He waves. "Bye-bye."

It's no use. You're trapped. Slowly you begin to feel your strength going. Your hair falls out, and then your blood boils. You finally understand what it must feel like to be an egg frying sunny side up.

The End

You join the expedition and prepare to leave the *Pole Star.* Mr. Bannon, the first mate, maneuvers the ship alongside the ice. The crew, using the deck cranes, off-loads the expedition's equipment.

Dr. Pogolsky's plan is to head south rapidly, about two hundred kilometers inland, and establish Camp One there. A prefabricated hut will be set up and stocked with supplies for the party on its return trip. The following morning, the expedition will head farther south and set up Camp Two on one of the lower peaks of the Rhumb Mountain Range, nearly four hundred kilometers from the edge of the ice pack. The ozone-monitoring equipment will be assembled and hooked up to a radio transmitter so that a continuous stream of reports can automatically be transmitted back to the United Nations ozone-monitoring station in New Zealand. Solar panels and batteries will supply the electrical power.

Dr. Pogolsky has given each person in the expedition flare pistols, rope, and a locator beacon just in case one of the snowmobiles breaks through the snow and falls into a crevasse. You shiver at the thought, and Uncle Ben sees your reaction. "That's one of the many risks in the Antarctic," he says with a grim smile.

You and the other members of the expedition kick-start your snowmobiles and attach the sleds that will carry the supplies and equipment across the ice. There are seven of you: three pairs riding tandem on the snowmobiles, with Uncle Ben towing a heavy sled of supplies on a fourth.

Turn to page 67.

With your heart in your mouth and the feeling that your back is going to be an awfully big target, you hunch over the handlebars and roar toward the Soviet station. Luckily the attackers don't spot you until it's too late. In minutes you're out of the range of their bullets.

You ride through the night, twice almost falling from the saddle from lack of sleep and fatigue. But by morning you can finally glimpse the coast, and then, only minutes later, the smoke from wood stoves rising in the still air.

You roar up in front of a complex of buildings. You try to stagger to the nearest door but fall on the snow from exhaustion.

Turn to page 91.

46

You tell your crew that you'll be following Scotty's plan. The *Terror* submerges and starts her run under the ice toward Chemsplat.

Twelve hours later, you notice the *Terror* is starting to angle up; then you feel the shock of two torpedoes being fired.

The intercom crackles. "This is Captain Hawk. We've blown a hole in the ice with our torpedoes. All hands stand by to surface."

It's time to act. You knock frantically on the door, and the guard opens it, his machine gun pointed at you. But he doesn't notice Scotty hiding behind the door. Scotty knocks him out from behind with a fire extinguisher.

You and your crew rush down the corridor to the engine room and open the salt water valves over the batteries. In seconds, salt water floods the batteries, and yellow chlorine gas begins to form. Warning alarms squeal. Your crew is prepared, having cut up blankets to use as temporary gas masks. You rush up a ladder to an escape hatch.

The hatch clangs back, and you and your crew make it out safely. All around the *Terror* are broken chunks of ice. By leaping from one floe to the next, you make it to solid ice. Looking back, you see men pouring out the conning tower of the *Terror*, choking on the gas.

You don't have much time. Soon they'll recover and be after you.

Turn to page 48.

You ignore the intrusion and begin to radio for help. You dial in the frequency of the New Zealand research station. You're about to call them when the microphone is knocked out of your hand by a huge, hairy fist. It's Igor!

"I've been looking all over for the two of you," he snarls. "The fact that you were trying to use the radio *proves* that you're both CIA spies!" He jerks you out of the chair by your collar. "I'm locking both of you up in a cell until I can get instructions from Moscow."

What's he talking about? Igor is out of his mind, and you and Sasha have got to get out of here to rescue Dr. Pogolsky's party. In desperation you turn and ram your head into his fat belly.

"*Ooooooph!*" he wheezes, staggering backward, the wind knocked out of him. Then he bounces off the wall like a rubber ball and comes rebounding back at you.

He collides with you, his hands windmilling, trying to grab you. You reel backward, trying to avoid his clutches. In doing so, you stumble over a thick black cable. You're falling, and your head collides with the electrical panel. Your head has smashed into a high-voltage connector, and the last thing you hear is a terrible ZAPPPPPP.

The End

48

You and your crew slow down to a jog as you cross the frozen plain, the wind snapping at your parkas. The temperature is mild for the Antarctic, only a few degrees below freezing, but you know as the day progresses the temperature could drop twenty or thirty degrees and you could all die unless you find cover.

Captain Hawk said that the Chemsplat research station was only a couple of kilometers away, located on a slightly mounded area.

"That must be it, skipper," Scotty says, pointing to a plateau rising up in the distance.

You and the rest of the crew climb up the final slope. But there's nothing there—no buildings, no vehicles, no generator exhaust stacks, nothing—only a slim flagpole with a strange flag whipping in the rising wind.

Next to the pole, you spot a depression in the snow with a rope trailing up out of it. You and Scotty heave on it, and slowly a trapdoor creaks open.

You have to get your crew out of the wind. Already their lips are turning blue with the cold. You take the lead, motioning everyone to follow you.

Turn to page 39.

Then Scotty yells to get your attention and points to the north. Something—a big fin?—is moving rapidly through the water, headed in your direction.

Not a whale! you hope desperately.

The lifeboats from the *Pole Star* are heavily loaded, and even a slight nudge by an inquisitive whale could capsize them!

But as the fin gets closer, you realize that it isn't a whale—it's a submarine's periscope!

Less than a hundred meters away, the sub surfaces, ballast tanks blowing, water streaming off her hull and conning tower. The hatches clang open, and the crew pours onto the deck.

You are preparing to welcome the submarine's crew when you see them holding machine guns, and pointing them directly at you!

Turn to page 13.

After several minutes of tense silence, you see the mercenaries from the submarine tromping toward the Chemsplat facility. Doktor Gribble pulls the trigger, and an intense red light beams out across the plateau.

Instead of vaporizing the crew from the submarine, Doktor Gribble uses the laser like a surgical scalpel, cutting a deep, circular trench into the snow and ice around them.

The mercenaries can't move. The trench is too deep and wide for them to cross. They fire a few shots from their rifles, then, one by one, throw their weapons down and put their hands up.

"That got their attention," Doktor Gribble laughs.

"You can't leave them out there!" you exclaim. "They'll freeze to death!"

Doktor Gribble grins, rubbing his hands together. "I wouldn't think of it, my friend. My men will throw them some tents and enough food for a week. Tomorrow I'll call the Americans on the radio and tell them where their spies are. By the time they get here, we'll be gone, because our work is almost complete."

Turn to page 89.

You wait for a minute without saying anything. Then—you're in luck! George, the Norwegian radio operator, holds up his hand. "I'll stay. My old back injury is acting up, and a few days rest will cure the problem."

You're both relieved and excited. Since you're an amateur radio operator, you can take over George's duties.

The next morning, you all head south on the three snowmobiles. It's a tiring ride, but the weather stays fair, and you make good time. By late afternoon, you can see the Rhumb Mountain Range and the glacier.

As you head on toward the mountain range, your snowmobile makes loud choking noises. You signal the others to halt as your engine sputters to a stop.

You're pretty sure the spark plugs need to be replaced. But when you explain to Dr. Pogolsky that it will take about an hour to let the engine cool down and replace the plugs, he shakes his head. "That wastes too much time. The rest of us will start up Mount Gay on foot carrying the equipment. Once you've fixed it, head for the glacier and park your snowmobile next to ours, then catch up to us on foot. You'll be able to rejoin us by evening."

It takes longer than you thought, but you're able to install the new spark plugs. Sure enough, on the first kick, your engine rumbles to life with a healthy growl.

Turn to page 79.

You'll need food for the trip back to the *Pole Star*. You carefully sift through the debris.

The emergency food ration box is the *only* one that hasn't been axed and then sloshed with gasoline. That's sort of odd, you think. You bend down and pick it up. Too late, you notice that there's a thin wire leading from the box to some kind of silver-colored cylinder that was hidden underneath the box.

Suddenly the cylinder splutters and then spurts a tongue of white flame. *WHOOOOMP.* The gasoline-laden fumes explode in a flash of sound and fury. Argggggggg! You always hated barbecues!

The End

As you open the control room door, a siren wails, lights flash. Workers, seated at consoles leap to their feet, their guns drawn.

A man rushes up to you. He is round and bald, and his eyes squint out from behind thick, amber-tinted glasses.

"I'm Doktor Gribble," he says breathlessly. "Who the blazes are you, and what are you doing here? This is a private research station owned by Chemsplat. You must go! *Immediately!*" He stamps his foot on the concrete floor.

"There's nowhere for us to go," you reply. "We're part of a United Nations team investigating the hole in the ozone layer. We're being chased by mercenaries from a submarine that broke through the ice less than two kilometers from here. They intend to come here to steal your research laser. They're armed and dangerous."

"How far are they behind you?" Doktor Gribble demands.

"An hour, maybe less."

"Fools and meddlers! Your footsteps in the snow will lead them right to us, but I'll take care of that. Follow me!" he commands.

Turn to page 58.

"Not if I can help it," you say between clenched teeth, settling in behind the laser. You turn down the power control to MINIMUM, then begin to fire short blasts at the mercenaries. As you suspected, the laser doesn't harm the crew from the *Terror*, but the intense light temporarily blinds them. In just a few seconds, the mercenaries are wandering around, their hands clasped over their eyes, going in circles and colliding with each other like a bunch of drunk penguins. Now that they're helpless, your crew jumps down to the ice to round them up.

You walk up to Captain Hawk. "So much for your evil plans of world domination," you say triumphantly.

"You don't understand," Hawk rasps. "Our instructions were to destroy the laser so that *no* country, even our own, would be tempted to use this evil technology for war. We've signed a treaty banning these weapons. Look in my jacket pocket. You'll find my orders."

Go on to the next page.

He's right. The orders are signed by the President of the United States!

Is Captain Hawk telling the truth, or are the orders clever forgeries? You want to believe him. If a dangerous weapon like the Chemsplat laser can be destroyed, the world will be a lot safer place. But while you were on the submarine, you were sure that Hawk planned to kill you and your crew. Now you're not so sure you can trust him again.

If you decide to trust Captain Hawk,
turn to page 60.

If you decide not to trust Captain Hawk,
turn to page 65.

Several tough-looking armed guards lead you and your crew down a steel tunnel, then up a set of stairs that lead to a small, circular platform. Doktor Gribble motions you toward the center of the platform. He seats himself in a bucket seat behind what looks like a telescope and raps out a command over an intercom. Machinery hums, and the platform begins to rise. Overhead the ceiling opens like a clamshell, revealing the dark blue of the polar sky. The platform keeps rising; then suddenly it stops, several meters above the level of the Antarctic plateau.

Doktor Gribble grips a control stick, which swings and lowers the tube so that it is aimed out at the edge of the plateau.

"What are you going to do?" you ask.

"Our Chemsplat intelligence service warned me that both the CIA and the KGB were planning to steal our research laser for their own nasty warmaking plans. Now they'll find out firsthand how good our laser is, because I'm going to stop all of them in their tracks."

If Doktor Gribble blasts the mercenaries from the sub, you and your crew will be saved. But on the other hand, once Doktor Gribble blasts them, he might swing his laser around and atomize you and your crew as well.

If you trust Doktor Gribble to save you from the mercenaries, turn to page 51.

If you think you and your crew should overpower the guards and take control of the laser, turn to page 68.

"Okay, Captain Hawk—you said you were ordered to destroy Chemsplat's laser. Now do it!"

Hawk smiles. From his backpack he pulls out a silver-colored tube, yanks a safety catch from it, then drops it down the opening in the laser.

"Let's get out of here fast." He grabs Doktor Gribble by the collar, and you all set off for the submarine.

As you run over the ice, Captain Hawk explains, "Gribble is a mad but brilliant scientist who developed the Chemsplat laser so that Chemsplat could burn holes in the ozone layer."

"But why would Chemsplat want to burn a hole in the ozone layer?" you ask.

Turn to page 80.

Signaling your crew to follow, you find a washroom. To their amazement, you pry a large mirror off the wall, then motion them to follow you back down the tunnel to the laser platform.

Just as you suspected, Doktor Gribble is manning the laser again. This time it's aimed at you and your crew!

"Stop where you are," Doktor Gribble commands, "or I'll zap all of you into a cloud of pink mist."

Turn to page 84.

You and your crew enter the door marked Power Generation Room. You pass through a second door, then a third, both very thick and built of a dull, soft metal.

Finally you are all standing in a concrete chamber. In front of you is a small dome with pipes leading into it and next to that something that looks like a swimming pool. The only strange thing about the swimming pool is that it glows with an intense blue light.

One of the crew suddenly grabs your shoulder. Her lips are trembling. "Now I know why there aren't any diesel generator exhaust stacks on the surface of the complex. They're producing electrical power with an unshielded atomic reactor buried under the ice. Another ten minutes in here and we'll all be fried like eggs."

Turn to page 43.

CAUTION

REACTOR PIT THIS SIDE TOWARD REACTOR

You yell at the top of your lungs—but you know it's too late for Dr. Pogolsky and his team to get out of the way of the tidal wave of snow that thunders down on them.

Oh no! you think. The figures in white have noticed you! Several of them raise rifles and fire. Bullets zing past you. They fire again, and this time their aim is much better. One bullet shatters the windshield of your snowmobile, another whistles through your backpack. There's nothing you can do for Dr. Pogolsky and the team right now. It's survival time!

You wheel your snowmobile around and head off to the east where there are a lot of ridges of ice in the snow. These ridges, called hummocks, will give you some protection while you figure out what you're going to do next.

Turn to page 87.

You still don't feel Captain Hawk can be trusted. Your crew rounds up the mercenaries and herds them back into the tunnel. But by then, Doktor Gribble has disappeared.

You need to lock up your prisoners for the time being so you can find Doktor Gribble and destroy the laser.

As you lead the group along the tunnel, you carefully check each room. One seems just right— a large underground kitchen. You rip out the telephone, break the light bulbs, and lock your prisoners inside the darkened room. One of your crew stays in the tunnel to guard outside the door.

"Next we have to find Doktor Gribble and figure how to destroy the laser, Scotty."

He nods. "Aye, skipper, but which should we do first?"

It's a tough choice. But two plans are beginning to form in your brain.

If you decide to deal with Doktor Gribble, turn to page 61.

If you decide to destroy the laser, turn to page 75.

The expedition makes good time over the glazed ice and hard-packed snow. The wind stings your face, and ice crystals form on your eyelashes as you ride along. But this is real adventure. You're paired with Sourdough, the oldest member of the expedition. But despite his age, he's strong and agile and a lot of fun. To pass the time, the two of you sing songs at the top of your lungs.

Turn to page 74.

Doktor Gribble moves the laser tube from left to right with his hand control, zeroing in on the mercenaries. You can't just allow him to kill them in cold blood.

You ease over to where Doktor Gribble is hunched down in his bucket seat, all of his concentration devoted to aiming the laser.

His finger is beginning to tighten on the trigger!

An idea comes to you. "Hit the deck!" you yell at your crew. They immediately fall flat on the platform. You yank at the hand control that makes the laser tube swing rapidly through a full circle. As it does, the end of the laser tube strikes the two guards who are still standing, knocking them unconscious.

Your crew quickly tie up the guards, and Scotty grabs a rifle and prods Doktor Gribble away from the trigger.

"You idiots!" Doktor Gribble moans. "Now they'll steal the laser—probably the most powerful weapon ever devised—and dominate the world. But you can be sure that they'll kill us first!"

Turn to page 56.

You volunteer to stay at Camp One, and you and Sourdough wave the expedition off in the morning. They'll be back in three days, and actually, you're looking forward to helping Sourdough with his survey of the mysterious Skull Mountain Range.

But after the expedition leaves, you realize that Sourdough doesn't seem to be all that happy to have you hanging around, and he keeps mumbling to himself about "tenderfoots who shouldn't be down on the Antarctic ice in the first place." And you thought he was your friend! Three days with this old codger is going to be *boring.*

By mid-morning, you both head west on skis toward the mountains. You're in the lead. A rope twenty-five meters long is tied both to your waist and to Sourdough's, just in case one of you falls through a snow bridge into a crevasse. The thought of something like that happening is more chilling to you than the bitter bite of the wind.

Turn to page 73.

You roar off on your snowmobile, heading north, trying to draw the skiers away from the glacier. Shots whistle past your ear, but they miss. When you're out of rifle range, you stop as if you were out of gas. You glance back with the binoculars. You were afraid that they would give up chasing you, but now they think they've got you. You wait just long enough, then start up again, drawing them farther and farther away, playing cat and mouse with them until late into the evening. When at last you lose them, you circle back to the glacier.

With your emergency locator beacon, you home in on your buried comrades. Working through the night, you shovel them out. By morning, everyone is saved.

Dr. Pogolsky is really upset. "All the scientific equipment, the radios, our food and survival supplies—everything—has been lost or is damaged beyond repair. Who were those dastardly people, and why did they try to kill us?"

You don't have any answers, but you do know that next time the group may not be as lucky.

Turn to page 90.

You take a fire axe from its bracket and start chopping at the cables. With only a couple of strokes of the axe, the cables part. Almost immediately, the alarm bell sounds, and Hans looks at you, obviously proud that you chose his solution.

But then you all notice that the *Terror* isn't turning in circles. It's nosing over into a deep dive!

"You fools," the intercom crackles. "This is Captain Hawk. You've cut the wires that control the diving planes. We can't keep the *Terror* level! She's headed for the bottom!"

Turn to page 34.

You and Sourdough are making good time across the ice shelf when suddenly the world falls out from underneath you! You've broken through a thin cap of snow that bridges a deep crevasse in the ice.

You tumble end over end, your skis breaking into splinters as you fall, your face and body smashing against the ice on either side of the crevasse until, with a snap of your safety rope, you jerk to a stop. The wind's knocked out of you; the pressure of the rope is like a vise around your waist. You hang there, disoriented, dazed, bobbing up and down like a puppet on a string.

Slowly your head clears. You're dangling by the safety line, with walls of ice well beyond your reach on either side of you. A little slit of daylight is far above you and the blackness below. Suddenly the rope jerks, and you drop even deeper into the crevasse.

Turn to page 81.

After eight hours of travel, Dr. Pogolsky calls a halt. The expedition force has traveled nearly 220 kilometers, and you're ready to rest. It takes another two hours to set up the prefabricated hut and stock it with gasoline, tins of food, and medical supplies for the expedition's return journey. Finally you finish building Camp One. You cook dinner, and Sourdough helps you wash the dishes. He's a funny old guy, you think, as you remember what Uncle Ben told you about Sourdough's background. He spent his early years in the Yukon and seems to know a lot about the Antarctic. He's the expedition's official surveyor and will stay behind at Camp One to keep an eye on things and do some surveying of the Skull Mountain Range, which is west of the camp.

Just before you turn in for the night, Dr. Pogolsky calls everyone together. "We've made good time today, and the weather forecast looks good for tomorrow. I think we should take just three snowmobiles on to Camp Two and leave the fourth one behind here. One of you will have to stay here with Sourdough. Do I have any volunteers?"

You'd really like to go on to Camp Two with the expedition, but maybe it would be more valuable to the expedition if you stayed behind.

---

*If you decide to stay at Camp One,
turn to page 69.*

*If you decide not to volunteer to stay,
turn to page 52.*

The Chemsplat laser is a tremendous threat to the world's population. But if you try to destroy it, a lot of people in the Chemsplat complex are going to get hurt. Hey! Wait a minute. You suddenly realize the laser is powered by electricity. If you can permanently destroy the power station, then the laser will be out of business.

You and your friends scramble back to the door marked Control Room. You approach a huge console with flashing lights and thousands of knobs and dials. Wow! That's why there were no generator exhaust stacks on the surface. Chemsplat's electrical power is generated by a nuclear reactor!

Suddenly a siren goes off, and a mechanical voice announces, "Attention. Unauthorized personnel in the Control room. Red alert—red alert!"

Any minute guards are going to arrive, and you had better get your act together.

Puzzling over the controls on the console, you notice two large red buttons, one marked Scram and the other one marked Flood. It looks to you as if one of the buttons might stop the reactor, but which one?

If you push Scram, turn to page 113.

If you push Flood, turn to page 107.

You start to swing back and forth, kicking your legs.

"Hang on!" Sourdough shouts down to you. *"Don't move!"*

For what seems like forever, you hang there on the safety line, slowly swinging back and forth like the pendulum on a clock. Then slowly, ever so slowly, inch by agonizing inch, you are pulled upward.

It takes more than an hour, but finally you're at the surface. Sourdough, his hands bloody from rope burns, helps you up from the lip of the crevasse, and both of you edge back from the chasm, then sit down and brew up some hot tea on your portable camp stove.

Sourdough nods toward his ice axe. "Old mountain climbing trick," he says. He goes on to explain that he was able to wrap six or seven turns of the safety line around the round wooden shaft of his ice axe, jam the end of the shaft into the ice, then rotate the metal end of the axe, slowly winding you up to the surface.

Now you know that he *is* your friend—for life— because he risked *his* life to save yours.

"We better get back to camp and get your hands properly bandaged," you suggest.

He nods, and you gather up your equipment for the trek back.

Go on to the next page.

It takes a long time to trudge back to the camp because you've lost your skis in the crevasse, but by late afternoon, you can see the hut in the distance.

But something's very wrong. Near the hut, there are ski tracks all over the place. Counting them up, you estimate that there were six or seven skiers in the party.

Sourdough rushes into the hut and yells from inside. Pushing open the door, you see that someone has taken an axe to your supplies, broken open the cases of food, then poured gasoline over the whole mess. The gasoline fumes are so thick that your eyes sting. It's a wonder the whole camp didn't burst into flames. Sabotage! But by whom?

Turn to page 82.

You remember that Dr. Pogolsky said he and the rest of the party would dismount at the glacier and climb Mount Gay, the peak on the right, until they were near its crest. With your binoculars, you can see the party heavily burdened with equipment, slowly toiling up the snow field. It will take you a couple of hours to catch up.

You scan around the glacier, trying to figure whether you can take a shortcut. And then, as you look higher up Mount Gay, you notice something moving. It's a figure in a white parka and pants— no, it's more than just one person. There are two, three . . . You count seven of them, and they're clustered in a small group above the crest of an overhanging snow cliff, right over Dr. Pogolsky's party. You have a sinking feeling in your stomach.

As you watch, there's a big puff of smoke, then the flash of a massive explosion. The figures in white have dynamited the crest of snow and started an avalanche!

Turn to page 64.

Hawk shakes his head, astonished that you couldn't guess. "Don't you know that when a person's skin is exposed to sunlight that hasn't been filtered by the natural ozone in the atmosphere, that person is exposed to dangerous radiation that will shorten life?"

You nod. "Of course. After all the research in the last few years, everybody knows that."

Captain Hawk is panting from the fast pace, but he continues to explain. "Chemsplat is building factories in every country in the world. Can't you guess what they're making?"

You shrug.

"Another brilliant product developed by Dr. Gribble—by far the best suntan lotion ever developed . . . and the most expensive. If the ozone layer had been destroyed, none of us could ever go outside without having to smear Chemsplat suntan lotion all over our bodies."

What a fiendish idea, you think. And from far behind you, there is a gigantic explosion. The Chemsplat laser is destroyed.

The submarine is in sight. You'll all be heading north out of the Antarctic toward home.

The End

You can guess what's happening, and it's not good. Sourdough is still on the ice cap, but your weight is slowly pulling him to the edge of the crevasse. The situation is desperate, and you don't have too much time to act.

By pumping your legs, you might be able to swing back and forth on the safety line and eventually reach the sheer wall of ice nearest you. Then, using the ice axe, you could chop hand- and footholds in the ice and relieve the load on the safety line, allowing Sourdough to dig in and drop a separate rescue line.

But looking down, you can see a shelf in the ice less than two meters below you. If you cut your safety line, you might be able to land on it and relieve the pressure. In seconds, Sourdough will be dragged to the lip of the crevasse, and you'll both be goners. You have to make up your mind fast!

If you choose to start swinging,
turn to page 76.

If you cut the safety line, turn to page 2.

"What do you think, Sourdough?" you ask, puzzled.

"Pretty plain to me," he says. "We've been bushwhacked, and if we'd been here, whoever it was would have probably killed us. I reckon, from the direction of the tracks, that after they left here, they headed inland toward Pogolsky and the rest of his team."

Somehow you've got to get word to Dr. Pogolsky! The only way is to ride through the night on your snowmobile and get to Camp Two before the killers do. But Sourdough's hands are badly cut up, and the emergency medical kit was destroyed by the invaders. Maybe you should take Sourdough back to the *Pole Star* where someone can bandage his hands. After all, he did injure himself saving your life.

If you take Sourdough back to the Pole Star, *turn to page 53.*

If you decide to warn Dr. Pogolsky, turn to page 86.

Professor Lazarev looks at Igor with disgust. "That's *your* part of the operation, and I can't over-rule you. But I *will* use the long-range radio to call the New Zealand base and ask them to fly to the glacier with a parachute rescue team. Once your helicopter is fixed, we can join them in the rescue effort."

"Nyet!" Igor shouts, his face black with anger. "The radio, as you well know, is to be used only by me to communicate with Moscow while I am here on my special assignment."

Sasha boldly steps forward and faces Igor. "I have been talking to our foreign friend, who tells me it's best to wait until the helicopter is repaired. Therefore, there's no need to call the New Zea-landers."

You told Sasha nothing of the kind!

"I'm glad that at least *he* has some sense," Igor says triumphantly. He turns and slams the door behind him. Professor Lazarev rushes after Igor, arguing that the repair work must be done as quickly as possible.

You're astounded and very angry. Every minute wasted decreases the possibility of getting Dr. Pogolsky's team out alive. And you're afraid you won't be getting much help here with Sasha and Igor interfering.

If you confront Sasha, turn to page 96.

If you rush outside, turn to page 94.

One of your crew raises his rifle, but you shake your head, then turn back to Doktor Gribble.

"You're finished, Doktor Gribble. Move away from that laser."

He laughs in an insane cackle and throws a switch. A deep throbbing sound begins, then a piercing whistle, which builds in pitch to an intolerable scream.

A strobe of blue light pulses from the laser. But you have raised your mirror so that it catches the laser beam and reflects it back at Doktor Gribble. There is a brilliant flash that dazzles your eyes. When you can see again, the laser has been turned into a blob of molten metal and glass, completely destroyed. And all that is left of Doktor Gribble and his evil plans is a puff of smoke.

The End

Sourdough is as tough as an old boot. His hands are hurt, but in a couple of days of easy skiing, he can make his own way back to the *Pole Star.* And you're sure he'll understand your decision. It's his life balanced against the lives of Dr. Pogolsky and his scientists. You explain your plan to Sourdough.

"Good luck, greenhorn," Sourdough calls after you as you mount up on your snowmobile. "I'll get back to the ship all right, so don't worry about me."

You wave and then blast off across the snow. You keep the throttle wide open, eating up the kilometers. You know that you're going dangerously fast, but you figure your enemies have a head start on you. You've got to beat them to Dr. Pogolsky!

Finally you see the Rhumb Mountain Range and the glacier.

Turn to page 79.

You make it to the safety of the ice hummocks. From your skiing experience, you know that most people caught in an avalanche can survive, so long as they're dug out by a rescue team within twenty-four hours. And each of the people in Dr. Pogolsky's party is equipped with an emergency locator radio beacon for just such a situation.

Maybe you can lead the people who tried to sabotage the mission on a wild-goose chase. They're on skis, but you're on a snowmobile that can go three times as fast. You decide you'll try to lead them *away* from the avalanche area, lose them by erasing your tracks, then circle back and rescue Dr. Pogolsky's party.

You quickly check your map. Less than five hours' hard riding from here, there's a Soviet research station, MIR. Dr. Pogolsky mentioned that some scientists there were doing work that had been tremendously beneficial to worldwide weather-reporting efforts. You wonder if those scientists could help you rescue the expedition.

You peek around the snow hummock. You can see the attackers. They're not walking down the glacier—they're skiing straight down it like wild demons. You've only got a few seconds to make a decision.

If you think you can shake off the attackers and then return to rescue Dr. Pogolsky's party, turn to page 70.

If you decide to go to MIR instead, turn to page 45.

Minutes later, you meet Sasha out at the dog kennels. The dogsleds have already been loaded with rescue equipment. As Sasha hooks up the dog-team harness, he suddenly frowns. "Suppose Igor finds out that we've gone and decides to follow us in the helicopter? That could be a real problem for us."

You hadn't given it much thought, but an idea comes to you. "Sasha—I can sabotage the helicopter but I'll need your help. If you can call the mechanic away from the hangar, I'll be able to find something to jam the blades with so that when the rotors start turning, the whole mechanism will self-destruct."

Sasha smiles at your plan. "I have another plan. Perhaps more simple," he says. "We could put sugar in the fuel tank and cause engine trouble."

If you feel destroying the rotors is the way to go, turn to page 101.

If you prefer Sasha's plan, turn to page 103.

Doktor Gribble leads you back into the complex. After a good hot meal, he expresses his thanks. "By alerting me to the CIA plan, you saved Chemsplat a lot of money, and we'd like to show you how grateful we can be. We'd like to replace the ship you lost."

Never one to look a gift horse in the mouth, you accept. After all, one good deed deserves another.

The End

Wearily you all head down the face of the mountain. The snowmobiles are operable, but the amount of gasoline in their tanks is low. Your spare cans of gas are somewhere up the mountain, buried under the snow. Your fuel will probably run out before you make it back to the ship.

Then you see a thin beam of intense bluish light slowly sweeping the sky. "A laser beam!" you say, astounded.

Dr. Pogolsky nods. "You're right. But a laser beam of that tremendous power would require a huge electrical generating plant. It must be some research facility that we don't know about. But they'll surely give us shelter and some assistance. Let's go. Without food, shelter, and more gasoline for our snowmobiles, we'll die trying to get back to the *Pole Star.*"

Soon you are heading eastward toward the beam. As you journey, you're careful to take a compass bearing, just in case the beam suddenly fades. And sure enough, by late afternoon, it disappears. You and the group carry on, following the compass course, hoping you can find the unknown research facility before evening. At times you don't know if your group will survive the exposure to the bitter cold and stinging winds after their harrowing ordeal.

Turn to page 102.

When at last you revive, there is a blur of faces leaning over you, the excited babble of voices, then gentle hands picking you up. In minutes you're inside the research building, a blanket tucked around you, a mug of steaming cocoa in your hands. Groggy from lack of sleep, you stumble through your story.

Professor Lazarev is the research station's chief scientist. He immediately barks out orders, and men scatter to round up rescue equipment, food, and medical supplies.

A younger man hands you a plate of hot stew and buttered black bread. "My name is Sasha. I'm Professor Lazarev's son. I'm in charge of the sled dogs," he says with modest pride. "Now eat up quickly. We'll be airborne in ten minutes." You realize that these people are doing everything possible to help you. It's a wonderful feeling to know that they really care.

Suddenly the door crashes open. A gigantic man stands there, his hands on his hips. "What's going on?" he demands.

"Captain Igor—I have no time to play your games," Professor Lazarev quickly explains. "We've got to take the helicopter on a rescue mission. Get out of my way!"

Igor smirks. "Think again, Professor. The helicopter has a serious technical problem that's being worked on by my mechanic. It won't be ready until I say it's ready. That's a bit of rotten luck, isn't it?" He laughs wickedly.

Turn to page 83.

You and Sasha dive behind the book cabinet. You hear the grate of footsteps on the floor, the snap of a switch, and then a barrage of radio static. The intruder begins to call another radio station, and you immediately recognize the harsh voice as Igor's!

The other station answers, but the static is so heavy that the voice is garbled and you can hear only Igor's side of the conversation.

"*Da*, of course I know. The young spy escaped and arrived here at the research station, asking us to form a rescue party. You bungling fools—you should have waited until this meddler caught up with the climbers and was buried alive with them in the avalanche." You peek out and see Igor's face is red with rage. "Now young Sasha, who may have been persuaded to their cause, is also missing. But I'll soon find them both and throw them in the cells," he says, laughing. "Then I'll fly out to the glacier in the helicopter to join you so that we can complete our mission. This is Igor signing off."

You can't believe your ears! Igor had something to do with creating the avalanche!

Turn to page 108.

You race outside looking for some form of transportation you can grab. Coming to MIR for help has been a waste of precious time. You realize you'll have to do this job yourself.

Off to your right you see a large shed. You run to it and carefully open the door.

Extraordinary luck! You see snowmobiles along with various other cold-weather vehicles such as snowplows and sleighs. In the corner, almost hidden from view, is a motorized hang glider!

Last summer you took lessons in hang gliding. You wonder whether you dare try it again without a refresher course. But you have to get back to Mount Gay as soon as possible.

Quietly you push the glider out of the corner, refuel it, and open the shed doors. Fortunately the engine starts right up, but the noise creates a tremendous racket. You're airborne in seconds. As you head south, you see people below waving madly, making signs for you to come back.

Turn to page 3.

You follow the others into the laboratory. The room is dark, but you can hear the sounds of animals moving around. And you can certainly smell them. Phew!

The door locks behind all of you, and suddenly the center of the room is flooded with blinding light.

"Ah . . ." says a voice from a speaker on the wall. "Visitors from the *Pole Star*. I'm Doktor Gribble, and you've meddled in my affairs once too often. Now you're meddling in Chemsplat's affairs as well."

Suddenly a steel cage drops from the ceiling, fencing all of your party behind steel bars.

Turn to page 99.

You grab Sasha by the elbow and pull him angrily aside. But Sasha turns to you and says, "Don't worry, I didn't betray you. Just keep quiet and follow me." He crooks his finger, beckoning you. You go into the kitchen, then through a door and down a flight of steps.

Sasha holds his finger up to his lips. "This tunnel connects all the buildings together so we can move around in blizzards without having to go outside," he whispers. "We have to get past Igor's command post without him or his men noticing."

"But where are we going?"

He smiles. "To where the long-range radio is installed, of course, so we can contact our friends, the New Zealanders."

You follow Sasha along the dark tunnel. Occasionally the tunnel branches off into stairs leading up toward the surface.

Sasha suddenly stops, his body tensing, then turns to you.

"Follow close behind me and keep very quiet. This stairway leads up to Igor's command post. He mustn't know what we're doing."

As you sneak past the stairwell, you can hear both Igor's voice and Professor Lazarev's raised in a heated argument. You want to eavesdrop, but Sasha grabs your arm and hustles you up the tunnel.

Go on to the next page.

When you're out of earshot, you stop Sasha. "What's going on here? One of the world's greatest scientists is buried under tons of snow, and Igor would be happy to let him and the others die!"

Sasha shakes his head sadly. "My father and his associates are respected scientists also. But Igor and seven of his men flew in from Moscow less than a week ago on some kind of secret mission. You have to understand, my friend, in every country of the world there are all kinds of people, some good, some evil. The world wants peace, but people like Igor do not. That's why I'm helping you."

You follow Sasha up a set of stairs and through a steel door. Inside is a room filled with electronic equipment, computers, printers, and a massive power distribution panel still in the process of being wired.

"This way," Sasha says, quickly leading you to the long-distance radio transmitting station. You're about to turn the radio on when you hear the crunch of heavy boots, then a key inserted in the door to the outside.

If you stand your ground, turn to page 47.

If you tell Sasha to hide, turn to page 93.

"I have developed the world's most powerful laser," Doktor Gribble cackles. "So powerful that I can destroy satellites at will. But for now—I am just burning holes in the ozone layer."

"But the sun's dangerous ultraviolet rays will penetrate the Earth's atmosphere! And millions of people will die of fatal sunburn!" You press against the steel cage, but the bars don't budge.

"Ah—but you're wrong. Chemsplat, the multinational chemical manufacturer that funds my research, has developed a very effective suntan lotion. Unfortunately, it's also very expensive. However, that's not my concern. If the six billion people of the earth don't want to die from the effects of sunburn, they will have to buy Chemsplat suntan lotion. And Chemsplat will make *billions,* thanks to me!

"And all of you will be my new experimental animals. Without the protection of Chemsplat suntan lotion, of course." As foil reflectors move into place, an overhead door slides open, exposing you and your friends to the bright Antarctic sun. But the air is bitter cold—and the temperature is dropping by the minute. You look around for some means of escape, but your cage is shut tight.

Your end reminds you of a TV dinner—you are going to be deep-frozen and broiled at the same time.

The End

Only seconds after you call, the New Zealand station answers. Without wasting time, you tell them that you're from the *Pole Star* expedition and that Dr. Pogolsky's party is buried in an avalanche on Mount Gay.

Suddenly Igor bursts in, pulls the power cord on the radio, and wrestles your arm behind your back, driving you in front of him toward the stairs that lead down to the tunnel. A couple of minutes later, he has thrown you into a cell.

Less than ten minutes later, Igor pushes Sasha into your cell.

One horrifying week later, both of you are flown to Moscow to be put on trial as spies.

Turn to page 111.

You tell Sasha you'd like to try to destroy the rotors. Sasha hastily walks into the hangar and tells the mechanic that Captain Igor would like to see him in his command post. You keep out of sight so as not to make the man suspicious, and when he leaves, you sneak in.

"Sasha, go outside and make sure to warn me if anyone is approaching," you say.

Last summer you worked at a local airport, and you know the perfect spot to jam the rotors! The damage will be so bad they'll have to order new blades from the Soviet Union.

Grabbing a sturdy screwdriver, you climb the fuselage.

You're standing there, leaning your elbows on the tops of the blades, when you hear the hum of the engine revving. Unable to believe it, you look over your shoulder and see Sasha locked in Igor's arms. Igor's hand is clamped over your friend's mouth!

The blades rotate. First one blade whacks into you, then another. What a way to go!

The End

Finally you spot a plateau, and all of you gather at the foot of the slope leading up to it. It's obvious that the frostbitten scientist and his assistants will not last out in the freezing atmosphere much longer. Shelter must be found—soon!

"We'll approach on foot," Dr. Pogolsky says softly. "We'd better not advertise our arrival, just in case . . ."

All of you are winded as you reach the top of the plateau. But there's nothing there—no buildings, no signs of life, nothing!

But Marie has excellent eyesight. She points to a pole with a flag on top of it sticking up out of the snow.

Cautiously you all approach it. Then you notice that there's a rope trailing up out of the snow next to the pole. You pull on it, and a door creaks upward, revealing a set of stairs that lead downward into a corridor. You've found shelter, at last!

Turn to page 110.

"Great idea," you tell Sasha. You head for the hangar while Sasha goes to the kitchen. Ten minutes later, he comes back from the kitchen with a bulge under his jacket, giving you a secret wink.

You distract the mechanic as Sasha sneaks up to the helicopter's gas tank and pours in the two-kilo bag of sugar.

Mission accomplished! Igor will be able to start the chopper, but he won't get far before the engine loses power and he has to land! He may catch up to you by snowmobile, but it will take much longer.

You and Sasha run to the kennels and on your way meet Professor Lazarev, Sasha's father. Professor Lazarev asks to join the rescue effort because he has always wanted to meet Dr. Pogolsky, a scientist whose work on the atmosphere is famous worldwide. So you, Sasha, and the professor head south toward the glacier on the sleds.

You make good time, driving through the night hours, arriving in the early morning.

After a desperate search, you find your uncle Ben, who's clawed his way up out of the snow. He's dizzy, confused, and half-frozen. You want to make him some hot soup on your camp stove, but he bravely shakes his head. "No. Find the others. I'll be all right," he says.

Turn to page 109.

As you wait in the corridor, out of the gloom rush a bunch of men in white snowsuits, guns held at the ready. "Comrade Captain Igor!" one of them shouts. "We have captured the enemy agents!" From around the corner comes the hulking figure of their leader.

"CIA spies!" Captain Igor shouts. "You thought you could steal the Chemsplat laser secretly installed here, but I've foiled you."

"What laser?" you ask. You hope to keep him talking while you think of a plan.

"Do you take me for a fool?" Igor snarls. "For months we in the KGB have known that Chemsplat has the world's most powerful laser. If it falls into the hands of a world power, then it will ruin all chance of peace. My country has signed a treaty banning the use of Star Wars weapons. We have been ordered to destroy the laser so that no one—not even the Soviet Union can steal it and use it as a weapon."

Turn to page 112.

106

Although you allow Igor and his KGB thugs to lead the way, you're really wondering whether they might secretly plan not to destroy the laser but to steal it, then turn it over to their military despite the peace treaty.

At your signal, you and your friends overpower Igor and his fellow agents, then herd them along the corridor until you find a large storeroom that contains supplies of food for the Chemsplat facility. You push them into the room, slam the door shut, and set a guard to make sure they don't break out. So far so good. Though the scientists are puzzled, you have no doubt about what must be done.

Turn to page 75.

BANTAM
SHOP~AT~HOME
C·A·T·A·L·O·G

Special Offer
Buy a Bantam Book
for only 50¢.

Now you can order the exciting books you've been wanting to read straight from Bantam's latest catalog of hundreds of titles. *And* this special offer gives you the opportunity to purchase a Bantam book for only 50¢. Here's how:

By ordering any five books at the regular price per order, you can also choose any other single book listed (up to a $5.95 value) for only 50¢. Some restrictions do apply, so for further details send for Bantam's catalog of titles today.

Just send us your name and address and we'll send you Bantam Book's SHOP AT HOME CATALOG!

CHOOSE YOUR OWN ADVENTURE

ABOUT THE AUTHOR

SEDDON JOHNSON grew up in Argentina and attended Randolph-Macon Woman's College in Virginia. She has taught English as a second language and the Montessori system to 3–12 year olds in Puerto Rico, Boston, and Vermont, where she presently lives.

ABOUT THE ILLUSTRATOR

FRANK BOLLE studied at Pratt Institute. He has worked as an illustrator for many national magazines and now creates and draws cartoons for magazines as well. He has also worked in advertising and children's educational materials and has drawn and collaborated on several newspaper comic strips, including *Annie*. A native of Brooklyn Heights, New York, Mr. Bolle now works and lives in Westport, Connecticut.

A mechanical voice announces, "Reactor scrammed and automatically shutting down. Electrical power being shut off."

The corridors of the Chemsplat station grow dim. The air is starting to chill because the heating units, powered by the nuclear reactor, are no longer working. Only minimum battery power is available now, and an order goes out over the public address system: "Evacuate!" Before long, the walls will be crusted with ice. Chemsplat will become a frozen grave.

The Chemsplat employees are already evacuating, taking with them just what they can carry. There probably wasn't enough time for them to send out a radio message. Without help, they'll have to walk all the way to the coast to be rescued.

In the dark, one of the Chemsplat guards rushes up to you, his flashlight already going dim. He has dynamite with a long fuse in his hand. "Why are you hanging around? We're blowing up the exits! This place and its secrets will be sealed up tighter than a tomb! Didn't you hear the order to clear out?"

You release your captives and with the others make it out just in time. A fleet of helicopters arrives and flies you all to safety.

The End

112

You're dumbfounded. The KGB working for peace, nor war!

"You're wrong about us being CIA spies," you argue. "We came to Antarctica on a scientific mission to learn about the depletion of the ozone layer. But I understand now why that's happening. The Chemsplat laser is so powerful that when it's pointed up at the sky, it destroys the ozone layer."

Igor's face is puzzled. But suddenly he grins. "Hokay. Prove that you're not CIA and help me destroy the laser."

Turn to page 106.

Through all of this, Sasha keeps telling you that it will turn out okay. But you're dubious, until the day comes when the General Secretary of the Soviet Union personally releases you both from prison. He apologizes, saying that Igor did not follow orders and has been reassigned to Siberia to count snowflakes for the next ten years. You also learn that Dr. Pogolsky's party were rescued and are already back at U.N. Headquarters with important new scientific data concerning the depletion of the ozone layer.

For the next month, as a guest of the Soviet Union, you and Sasha tour the country.

The End

You and your party descend the stairs, past a room where cold-weather clothing is hung, down a dimly lit corridor. No one has stopped you yet: no guards, no welcoming party, no one! It's as if the whole underground complex were deserted.

Finally you come to a three-way branch in the corridor, each with a door. One is marked Laboratory, another Power Generation Room, and the third Control Room.

Dr. Pogolsky grabs the handle to the door marked Laboratory. "This way," he urges. "There will be scientists like us working in there, people who speak our common language of research, people we can trust to help us."

But from somewhere up the corridor, you suddenly hear footsteps running toward you. They could be coming to welcome you—but then again, they might be unfriendly.

If you decide to enter the laboratory, turn to page 95.

If you wait to see who's coming down the corridor, turn to page 105.

With the help of your locator beacon, you find the others and dig them out. They are roughed up and have minor frostbite on their toes and fingers but are otherwise all right.

"We must get to a shelter immediately so that they can warm up," Professor Lazarev says.

"But where?" you ask. Except for going back to the Soviet base or the *Pole Star,* there's nothing within hundreds of kilometers.

"There is a place," says the professor. "Our satellites have finally located the Chemsplat station. It's run by dangerous and greedy people, but it's our only choice."

Doubling up on the dogsleds, your party heads toward Chemsplat, using Professor Lazarev's map coordinates. The dogs are winded, even though Sasha urges them on.

As your party approaches a frozen plane of ice and snow, Professor Lazarev signals for the dogsleds to halt. "According to my information, this is the location of the Chemsplat station," he says. The dogs are reined in, the sleds are unhitched, and Sasha feeds the animals.

Dr. Pogolsky and Professor Lazarev pace back and forth through the crunching snow, arguing.

You pull your parka close around your neck. As cold as you feel, you know the others are worse off after being buried alive. Still, none of you can survive much longer without food and warmth.

Turn to page 102.

You catch your breath as Igor stomps past your hiding place and out of the room, banging the door behind him.

Sasha is terribly upset. "So my father was right. Igor and his men are KGB spies." He glances at his watch. "Igor never planned to allow us to use the helicopter. The only way we can save your friends is to use my dogsleds. We can have them loaded in minutes. I'll tell my father first and then meet you over near the kennels." Sasha runs out to prepare the sleds.

Maybe you should still contact the New Zealanders. After all, they can fly to the glacier in only a couple of hours and get started on the rescue well before you and Sasha could arrive by dogsled. But Igor's men might hear your broadcast and be waiting to shoot down the New Zealand plane when it arrives at the glacier.

If you call the New Zealanders, turn to page 100.

If you take the dogsled, turn to page 88.

You push the Flood button. A loud horn starts squawking a warning. Then the mechanical voice says, "Attention all personnel. Fire in the reactor room—fire in the reactor room. Watertight doors are now sealing off the complex and flooding of the reactor is now starting. Evacuate the complex. Repeat, *evacuate the complex!*"

You and your friends are startled as massive steel doors bang down, and streams of water gush from overhead pipes.

Ice-cold water is rising around your feet, then over your legs. You pound on the doors, but they won't budge. The lights on the console are going crazy, flashing like a pinball machine gone berserk. Then a panel lights up with the message, *REACTOR FLOODED. PROCEED WITH PUMPOUT PROCEDURE.*

But try as you might, you can't find any operating manual. The water is now over your waist and rising rapidly. Electrical circuits are shorting out in showers of sparks.

The water's over your shoulders now. Then over your head. The worst thing is that you always hated cold showers. At least this will be the last one you'll ever have to take.

The End